To Testify from the Grave

Richard Anthony Sattanni

America Star Books

First printing

America Star Books has allowed this work to remain exactly as the author intended, verbatim, without editorial input.

Softcover 9781630844875
PUBLISHED BY AMERICA STAR BOOKS, LLLP
www.americastarbooks.com

Printed in the United States of America

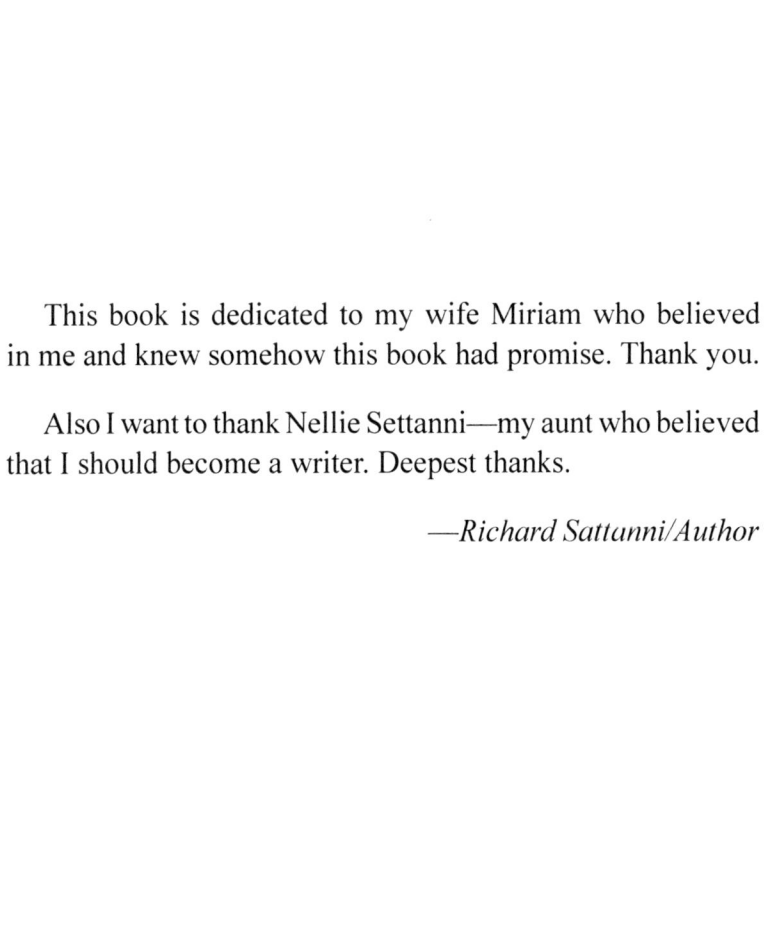

This book is dedicated to my wife Miriam who believed in me and knew somehow this book had promise. Thank you.

Also I want to thank Nellie Settanni—my aunt who believed that I should become a writer. Deepest thanks.

—*Richard Sattanni/Author*

TO TESTIFY FROM THE GRAVE

PART 1

THE body of SANDRA MARIE STEWART laid there bloody and her torso smashed open due to the fall from the sixteenth floor. The police arrived quickly, along with the coroner as well as the C. S. I. force to try to figure out if this was an accident or a murder. IT would be days before this crime could be figured out, maybe even weeks to do a thorough investigation. SANDRA MARIE STEWART had been at the casino hotel for a board meeting with her tycoon of a husband the head of a prestigious marketing firm who was at a convention for major companies to meet to discuss the economics of the business world. Sandra and her husband BLAKE had been married three years now with one daughter LOUISE just turning two years old the upcoming SATURDAY.

Now by a turn of fate LOUISE had become motherless that morning. IT was a horrible sight as the blood still flowed from the victim's mouth and body. The police disbanded the crowd and the murder or fall was under investigation. The C. S. I.

TEAM went right to work. The detectives now questioned SANDRAS' husband BLAKE. BLAKE told his side of the story but, had a real good alibi.

HE claimed to be in the casino's men's' room with a gay friend of his at the time that SANDRA had fallen from the window. His friend swore they were having sex during that time and there were no other witnesses so BLAKE EDWARDS was out of the picture at least for now. The police had led an investigation for months later and the case closed. The final outcome SANDRA'S death was ruled a suicide and BLAKE EDWARDS was a free man in the eyes of the law.

A few years passed and BLAKE EDWARDS started to date a teacher he had met. Their relationship got serious and they were married. His second wife had no idea that BLAKE was bi-sexual and that he had a male lover. The marriage lasted only two years due to her death. Her body was found by the upstairs maid while BLAKE was away on a business trip. BLAKE and his wife KATHY had had a falling out a month before her death. BLAKE'S male lover begged BLAKE to kill his wife due to jealousy by REX his lover. BLAKE first said no but then REX put pressure on him so BLAKE hired a professional killer for quite a bit of cash to rub her out. So BLAKE and his lover were in ENGLAND the hit man got to her and cut her throat while she was asleep-one night.

The neighbors found her bloody body and notified the police. Again after a lengthy investigation BLAKE EDWARDS was not held at all responsible because of his alibi. The hotel verified that he was indeed there during that time period and day. SO again he was off the hook with the law.

KATHY had friends and family that felt BLAKE had hired someone to kill her but evidence led back to her tycoon husband. Plus none of her family had the money to hire a private investigator to prove otherwise. BLAKE went on to enjoy life searching again for a female partner to cover up his affair with REX his Gardner. HE had to hide the truth.

The wives were taken as a lover of some kind but his true love was REX who he had had an affair with for several years now. NO one ever suspected them as lovers for they were extremely discreet about their relationship. A few years passed and BLAKE EDWARDS was on a trip to FLORIDA but alone this time. REX had been ill possibly with aides so he was in a hospital at that point.

A short time later BLAKE went to his hotel after leaving the airport. HE now had signed the registry and went to the elevators to get to his room. AS fate would have it he struck up a conversation with a BEVERLY MARLOWE, a lawyer from NEW YORK CITY. HE asked to meet him later for a drink at the bar and she accepted. HE found his room and with the flash card opened the door. The room was expensive but the view was stunning. The white and tan long drapes along with the red carpeting added a EUROPEAN touch and the sun warming the large room added warmth to its' elegance. HE unpacked, undressed, showered and wrapped a white terry towel around his waist as he poured himself a complimentary wine into the chilled glass HE reached for his cigarettes and lit one. HE laid back on the oversized water bed. HE was starting to think about the woman he had met on the elevator. AS far as he was concerned she was very hot looking. She was tall, all legs like the saying goes, blonde hair and blue eyes with a body like a magazine model She was his dream girl at least for tonight. Sure he thought about bringing her to his room for some adult games but that perhaps would be his night cap.

Blake looked at the clock on the TV. IT was nearly seven p. m. HE dressed picking out his best shirt and slacks and sport coat. HE wanted to impress this babe and perhaps land up in bed with her for fun and games only grownups play. HE grabbed his cigarettes and his lighter and his room key and headed out the door to the elevator. IT was close to seven as he arrived on the lower level at the elegant lounge. The band was playing soft romantic music as BLAKE spotted her waiting at a small table. She motioned him over and he sat down quickly. She introduced herself as BEVERLY. BLAKE had no idea she'd be wife three in the future. They chatted and sipped martinis for a couple of hours and finally he suggested to go to his room for a bit more privacy. She jumped at the chance. She figured he wanted sex but so did she. She had not been with a man for two years since her husband had died suddenly from heart failure as they were on a cruise in the BAHAMAS. She had not even tried dating so she was wide open for a night in the sack with this handsome stranger. HE looked very rich in his LONDON FOG jacket and his PIER CARDIN shirt and fine slacks and his expensive shoes. HE wore a nice fragrant after shave lotion very enticing to the opposite sex.

BEVERLY held his hand as they waltzed sort of to the waiting elevators. She smiled at him as the doors closed and it motioned to the third floor. HE was starting to feel the effects of the booze as they stepped from the confines of the elevator crashes was starting to want him as she gazed into his room and he flashed the card and they entered the splendid room.

She was surprised at the elegance of his room versus her less expensive one. She gazed around the room eyeing the furniture and noticing the large water bed where she no doubt would spend the night with her knight in shining armor. She was amazed by his smooth manners and his generosity. She had no idea that he was a marketing tycoon, the sole president of a soap company that he started right out of college with some cash his deceased parents left him in a will. They had died just before his graduation in a fire at their condo in FLORIDA.

BLAKE had been an only child and the will covered all the goodies in his favor. HE took the cash and got into the soap business building a multi million dollar business in a matter of a few years. YES life was good for BLAKE. HE had the world by the ass and he knew it too. BEVERLY had no idea that she would rock his world and in a short time he'd propose to her. After several weeks of dating BLAKE gave her a beautiful diamond ring. She accepted his proposal to his surprise and they flew to VEGAS to be married in a small chapel there.

Their marriage lasted for a few years until he grew tired of her. She didn't keep her self looking good and she gained a few pounds due to his disappointment. Blake started sleeping with REX a few nights a week. REX satisfied his sexual appetite and BLAKE started to show less attention to BEVERLY. She started drinking heavy and started to pick up guys for one nighters so their marriage fell apart. Then one night as she was bathing in the gold figured tub BLAKE opened the bathroom door and threw into the tub an electric fan that right away hitting the water electrocuted her. HER body slumped in the water.

Blake panicked and called REX to come help him dispose of the body. REX arrived panting and out of breath and nervous as can be. They took the body down to the nearby river and dumped it off the bridge into the deepened blue colored water overshadowed by the moonlight. Her body went right to the bottom. The water swallowed her up and that was that. BLAKE laughed as he saw the bubbles rise to the surface. REX could care less for now he had BLAKE all for himself to indulge in his sexual escapades. A fisherman snagged her body a few days later with a fishing hook. Again an investigation occurred but BLAKE and REX covered their alibi. The police bought the story how she had gone out with different guys and was now lately being pimped by a black man who ruled the game of prostitution in town. The cops bought the story hook, line and sinker. REX laughed when he saw the headlines on BEVERLY'S death. HE could give a dam. HE was glad the bitch was gone. BLAKE felt relief that BEVERLY was gone. After sometime BLAKE got back into the dating circle. A few doors away a couple of twin sisters were moving in to a condo they had purchased together. JOANNA DEPORTE and her twin sister EILEEN now were practically his neighbors. The twins settled in and in a week or so were sunbathing in the nude on their private deck.

Meanwhile BLAKE using his pair of field glasses was scanning the area from his balcony Within minutes he was focused on the two twins. They were true blondes, with long legs, both stood six feet tall with bodies a man would kill for. BLAKE was in the mood for sex but not this time with REX. BLAKE sought sexual release of any kind as he viewed their tantalizing bodies, HE was duly exciting watching the twins kissing each other in ways that a man would caress a woman. This went on for a while as they held each other in intimate embraces. Finally tired of viewing the gals he focused on his other neighbors who had left their curtains open as they made love on the couch.

BLAKE wanted so bad to hit on JOANNA DEPORTE one of the sexy twins but could not figure out how to meet her. HE figured someday, somehow figure it out. BLAKE could not get her gorgeous body out of his mind. HE wanted her body so bad he could nearly taste her soft smooth skin. IT seem time passed quickly for BLAKE. His former wife BEVERLY was buried and he shrugged his shoulders as he read her obituary. Blake was glad she was dead and gone. She had gotten in his way with he and REX's affair. REX could care less about her. HE and BEVERLY had no use for each other. There was no doubt they had hated each other. IT truly was a known fact with those two that they would never ever have respect for each other. Anyway she was gone and out of their way and once more BLAKE walked away from the law due to insufficient evidence.

Weeks passed and BLAKE had forgotten all about JOANNA. With SUMMER in full swing he decided to head to the beach one afternoon, HE paid the parking fee and drove into the circular parking lot. The sun was real bright and warm breezes caressed his rugged complexion as he grabbed his multi-colored towel, his radio and his picnic basket. HE strolled along the pave walkway eyeing the young girls in their itsy bitsy bikinis. HE liked to look at the real young ones. it turned him on. Then he spotted an opening on the beach under a nice sized tree. HE sat down and unraveled the towel and opened his basket and pulled out a soda. HE would prefer a beer but no alcoholic stuff was allowed on the beach. HE gazed around the beach line with his field glasses. After a few minutes he spotted JOANNA DEPORTE lying there a few feet from him and she was alone.

After a while he figured he could casually go up to her and start a conversation. HE hesitated to approach her but then gambled that it was now or never. She unloosened her bikini top as she laid on her stomach. BLAKE was fascinated with her beauty. She was beyond beautiful. her jet blue eyes, her long tanned legs. her blond hair falling to her shoulders made quite an impression on him. HE hurried over as she laid there so quietly listening to her potable radio as the ocean caressed the beach. HE stood over her smiled and went onto introduce himself. She surprised him with a smile and she did not hesitate to speak which floored BLAKE right away. She invited him to sit beside her as she leaned on her hip. HER huge breasts were heaving up and down and her nipples were erect.

BLAKE tried to ignore her hot body which had his total attention now more so than ever. HE wanted those legs wrapped around him in a compromising position. HE was starting to feel a sexual need as he gazed at her large breasts with her hard nipples pointing straight at him. She felt comfortable knowing he was checking her body out as though she was in a secret fantasy world and that they had met before and that they were lovers now. She felt her heart beating faster than usual. HE admired her beauty and wanted a taste of her pretty red lips and to be taken deep inside her would be the ultimate rush. She reached out and touched his hand. HE smiled nervously as his hand felt the warm glow of her touch. HE could not believe what was happening. IT was if time stood still as they touched and kissed for the first time. She leaned even closer to him now. HE whispered to her hoping she'd say yes to go back to his place for a drink. She said yes and surprised him. His heart was beating like a base drum as she stood up and grabbed her gear and motioned him to take her home. They walked hand in hand back to his car. They drove off to his house on the beach that he used for these special moments of bliss.

AT his condo REX waited patiently for his lover to return home. Hombre would have to wait while BLAKE took his bisexual wants with a woman of such great passion with needs that he could duly satisfy. They drove without too much conversation. She seemed comfortable with him. HE could not wait to get her home to show her what passion he wanted to share with her. IT was a short drive back to his place. She eyed him as he drove his black CADILAC along the winding beach road. Finally they arrived at his place on the shore. HE parked his SEVILLE and opened her door for her. She smiled as he took her by the hand and helped her up the few steps to his lavish beach home. The waves of the ocean cracked hard against the rocks adding a romantic touch.

HE opened the red door and they entered the foyer. The living room was very large with white drapes and red carpet that filled the entire floor area. The bamboo bar was tucked away in one corner with tall bar stools to match. The basic furniture was of white leather, a couch and love seat joining each other and a fireplace that gave the room that certain touch. IT was a romantic setting for what they had in mind. She could not believe how beautiful the place was. HE took her towel from her and went to the bar. HE mixed two drinks and handed her one to her gently as though she was a princess in a fairytale. She was amazed at his manners. NO one ever treated her like this ever. She felt perhaps she had met her soul mate for sure not realizing that he had killed three prior wives. She gave into his advances and they made romance come to life on the waterbed in the next room. She felt loved really loved for the first time in her life. This was real she said to herself not a dream, not a fairy tale but reality in a beautiful setting. They made love for hours as the ocean pounded its' salty waves against the rocks on the ledges below the house.

BLAKE made two more martinis for them as he kissed her lightly as he returned to the bedroom a little exhausted but feeling real good about what took place. IT was about midnight now as they talked a little about how they had met that afternoon. She was trying to appear shy as she laid naked in his arms resting her head against his hairy chest. HE took her glass and poured two more drinks for them.

She decided to spend the night with him. HE was ok with that after all that was part of his plan anyway. HE got up and went to light the fireplace to eliminate the chill in the rooms. IN a short span of time the warmth of the fireplace filled the air with the warmth that added atmosphere more so to the romantic moments that they were sharing. JOANNA was as ready as she could be waiting to see what his next move would be BLAKE made his first advance towards her caressing her intensely. She just about melted in his arms. HIS eyes glowed so brightly, her lips parted warmly, her inner thighs trembled as he kissed her warm. waiting mouth. She was excited as he laid down next to her on the cool water bed. His hands moved in unison making her pant with desire. IN seconds they were in a intimate position both of them panting like two cats in heat. They made love for an hour without stop. She needed a breather now for at least a few minutes so he relaxed and laid beside her

TO TESTIFY FROM THE GRAVE

PART 2

HE wasn't happy with this outcome at all but did not say a word to break the romantic emotion. HE kissed her without force as she rolled over on her stomach. She was stirred up ready for another bout of mad passionate love. BLAKE seemed to gain some untapped energy and took her at once again giving his attention to all parts of her gorgeous body. BLAKE had dozens of lovers in his time so he knew how to create spark where needed too. HE made women beg for him by his attentiveness. JOANNA was truly a really perfect lover for BLAKE. She pleased him like no other woman ever did or tried to. BLAKE felt that this was more than a one night stand.

They made love through out the night several times. She seemed to not get enough of him no matter how much they went at it. She needed more. Finally the morning arrived. The sun focused a shadow of light over the beach house. The ocean rustled on the shore and warm breezes filled the air.

She was already lying there nude in BLAKES' massive arms. She smiled to herself as she realized they had spent their first night together. She needed to shower to rid her body of sweat and body fluids and the smell that traced in the air making her feel dirty. She hesitated to move from his grasp-it just felt so inviting, so good. so cuddly and of course so romantic. Her body tingled with the tantalizing sensation of wanting more hot sex was like a female cat in heat, truly caught up in a moment of lust. HE was pleased with how much endurance she seemed to have. She wanted to please him even though this could very well be a one nighter. HE sure wanted to see her again perhaps for a relationship of some sort. They laid there naked on the water bed talking like old friends. They found they had a lot in common. She told him she hadn't had sex in two years due to her fiancé was killed overseas in the line of military duty.

HE was surprised how well they got along. HE told her he'd like to be her steady guy from this point onward. She agreed instantly to that suggestion. With that said they had sex again. this time it was with more meaning than before. AT the end of the night BLAKE had convinced her to give up her place and move in with him at the beach.

BLAKE figured to let REX his male lover live in the condo in the city. HE could carry on his love for REX and JOANNA would not have to know about REX at all. He had the perfect plan but REX may not dig the idea so well for REX was a jealous guy when it came to BLAKE. JOANNA now made plans of moving in with BLAKE within the next two weeks or so which BLAKE was alright with that idea.

They had a couple of martinis and then proceeded to have more sex. She seemed to be in need of a man more than his former lovers. She was hot to the touch and BLAKE was loving every minute of it regardless how tired he was getting. IT was already five a/m when they went to sleep. BLAKE was exhausted and she just relaxed in his muscular arms and asleep in minutes.

Morning arrived BLAKE and JOANNA were still asleep in each others' arms. The sun was peeking through the drapes and the ocean was beating against the rocks and a warm breeze flowed through the open window. The sound of seagulls filled the morning air and a few youngsters headed down the rocky slope to the waters' edge.

Blake's cell phone rang breaking his sleep. He picked up the phone to find out it was REX calling about getting the black MERCEDES serviced BLAKE gave him the okay and hung up. HE looked over his shoulder at JOANNA lying there nude just waiting to be taken again into his arms and have a good morning love session. She would be more than willing to make love early in the morning to get her day started with an adrenalin rush.

She more than likely would like him to caress her softly until she could handle no more and get into the position to have torrid sex. BLAKE laid there next to her. Her hot body glowed in the light of the fire in the fireplace. She was hot to the touch just the way BLAKE wanted her to be. HE caressed her warm body and was turned on instantly. HE wanted to wake her but instead started to feel all over her body. JOANNA opened her sleepy eyes slowly and reached out and pulled him on top of her. IN minutes they were engaging in heavy sex as like two people on a blind date that went wild for some reason. For a while they seemed they were alone in the world captivated by pure lust.

BLAKE was now losing control as he roughed housed her without thinking. Oddly enough she loved having rough sex. The love session went on for hours without stop as though they were in a sex marathon of some sort. Finaly BLAKE was near exhaustion and she said she was getting sore so they quit and rested. They sat there chatting nicely like two old friends at a highschool reunion. They laughed and joked and talked about how they met and how much they enjoyed each others' company. BLAKE figured somehow in the future she'd be wife number four. HE had not told her yet about his prior marriages., She may not be to happy with the news of his prior marriages. HE was not ready to dump that bit of news on her. HE was only at this point interested in sex.

She had not questioned anything about his past. She had no way to know he was a killer and that he had beat the law thre times already due to lack of evidence. BLAKE played the loving partner and he convinced her that he was indeed a caring individual. The bottom line was that they were sexualy compatible and that mattered most to them at this point in time.

She had needs to be satisfied and vice a versa. Their lovemaking was if they had been together for years and knew each others' wants and needs. BLAKE had a way with women. he always did since his highschool days at BRODERICK HIGHSCHOOL. HE never had a steady gal until years later when he got finished with his studies. HE had married young and his first wife was barely out of her teen years when they tied the knot.

BLAKE was a father already at twenty one years old. A year later their baby died from a rare blood disease. With other wives there were no further births. BLAKE preferred not to have any more kids after he lost his only son which finished his desire to have others. HE liked life in the simple form. A wife, sex, and homes and fancy cars and lots of money were his only concerns.

BLAKE had come from a rich family. HIS father had owned a few franchises in a well known donut shop business and had made millions in the stock market when the market was thriving. Now he lived pretty much off the interest of his inheritance. His dad and mom were killed when their private aircraft had crashed somewhere in the PACIFIC. HE was an only child and the will read everything left to him. HE had the world by the ass, and he knew it to. Now here he was in a beach house with a beautiful woman without a care in the world. She had no idea how rich he was. IF they married she'd be set for life.

Cash was in abundance, stocks were making dividends c/ds were paying wellso life was great at least. HE had no intentions of marrying again at least not right away. BLAKE made two martinis as they sat and sipped their drinks the night moved in. The moon shed its' light overshadowing the roof of the beach house. There was a chill in the air as rain started to fall. IN a brief time the rain became a heavy downfall-and thunder filled the air with its' crackling sound and lightning seemed to be flashing everywhere. BLAKE closed the window and locked the patio doors. HE mixed two more drinks and then lit the logs in the hearth of the fireplace. IN a short time they were enjoying the brisk heat as the logs crackled end popped. They took a break from their sex capades for now. She was starting to get sore from to much activity. HE was getting a sore tip from to much sex also. They were definetly sexualy compatible and they realized that right away.

BLAKE and JOANNA showered together now and decided to have sex again as the water burst warmly onto their already heated up bodies. Her reactions to his caresses sent her over the edge to multiple orgasms like she never ever experienced before. HE was loving every minute grasping at her like a bull in heat, wanting to enter her backside which was how his former wives endured their sexual encounters in the past. JOANNA was real hot between her legs. Her womanhood glowed with need from her male counterpart. HE wanted to please her in every way possible. Finaly the love session came to a halt. HE was spent, it was useless to try to make love again. IT was truly over for him at least. JOANNA was still trying to get one more orgasm.

HE fingered her trying his best to get her to release but it was hopeless for her now. Plus her being tired didn't help. They showered again rinsing off the smell of body fluids and sweat. They toweled then went back to the bedroom. They both felt real tired but, both of them felt closer together now. BLAKE mixed two drinks and kissed her breasts as he handed her a drink. She smiled as she watched her nipples swell up. HE looked at her large breasts and then his eyes dropped to her pretty crotch.

She spread her legs open as wide as she could giving him full view of her wet vagina. HE touched her genital area running his fingers through her hairy bush. She was starting to get hot and pressed his long fingers deep inside her. HER body now shook with an excitement leading up to a climax that would be earth shattering. IN no time they were in a comfortable position. HE was ready for whatever she expected or wanted him to do to satisfy her sexual needs. HE moved his hands over her body with the precision of a surgeon. She started to breathe deeply and with a desire that he had never experienced before. HE had a hunch that she was going to be wife number four. HER sexual pattern was relative to his. They could not get enough of each other.

IT was around noon when they took a break from their sexual games. She told him that she was getting sore from to many hard thrusts. HE understood because he had been married a few times. HE knew women could not make love for a unlimited time slot. They rested now and talked on an intimate level each letting the other know what they expected in a bedroom setting. HE had no trouble telling her that oral sex on her and him was what he'd enjoy more than anything else. She smiled and explained honestly that she had performed oral sex numerous times on her deceased husband. She had no problem giving or receiving oral sex. BLAKE indeed now recognized her as a great candidate for wife number four.

They sipped their drinks for a while and made small talk. She told him she was born in BRITISH COLUMBIA but, was raised in the U. S. A. when her dad was in the military returned to the states again. HER mom had been a teacher in a elementary school back in ALABAMA. Her dad finaly was stationed at an airbase in his homestate of ALABAMA. JOANNA and her twin sister were raised in MONTGOMERY. ALABAMA. She later went to college in L/A. She had met DERRICK her former husband at school. HE was a coach for the football and basketball teams. They dated briefly and were married within a year or so after they met at the welcome home to the king and queen of the college. This was a tradition that the school had carried out since the early fourties. DERRIK had a good job teaching, while JOANNA did waitress work at a local run down bar. DERRICK hated JOANNAS' job. She also danced topless at the bar when asked to do by the mob. She was to frightened to say no to them so she worked the dance floor as well. She made good bucks dancing and once in a while she did lap dancing which DERRIK despised. A couple of of times DERRICK came to the club already drunk he started trouble with JOANNA as well as her kid sister. HE was over protective with JOANNA and eventualy she was fired due to his coming in the club and being abusive.

Now DERRECK was gone and nearly forgotten. Now she had a chance to land a new guy and start over, be more attentive to her male counterpart where necessary. BLAKE refreshed their drinks. She watched him walk to the bar his penis dripping and dangly loosely. She was amazed at the size of his penis. HER husband had been much smaller but his tip she felt had been wider than BLAKES'or was it simply her imagination dur to ectasy now taking hold of the situation. BLAKE handed her her drink and proposed a toast to the two of them to celebrate a new beginning. She reached out and touched his glass with hers. They chatted for a while longer, sipping their cocktails in between. HE then suggested to shower and head to the beach for a picnic.

They showered but did not make love this time around. She was to sore and he was to tired. They dressed casualy having their swimsuits on under their outer clothing. IT was off to the beach now to enjoy a day in the tropical like sunlight. HE started the black MERCEDES and they headed onto the main street. IT was a short drive to the PAVILON PARKabout four miles from his home. The park attendant collected five dollars at the gate and then they headed towards the beach wall looking for a parking place. Someone pulled away now BLAKE took the unoccupied space. HE took her by the arm and carried the small picnic basket as well. There was very little sand space left but they managed to find a quaint spot. They put their towels on the sand and took their clothes off and got ready to take a swim. The sun was shining and a warm breeze filled the air as the ocean kissed the shoreline with its'heavy waves. IT was truly a typical summer day. They splashed each other playfuly and then BLAKE picked her up and tossed her into the water surprising her to say the least. She regained her position and they laughed and tossed water at each other like two small children. After an hour of playfulness they decided to have their picnic lunch. BLAKE opened the basket and handed her a roastbeef sandwhich on a hard roll along with a soda.

She smiled at him as she unwrapped the sandwich. BLAKE smiled warmly at her realizing to himself only how much JOANNA looked like his first wife. They sat and talked and listened to the radio. After chatting for at least an hour they decided to go for another swim. The sun was going down now and the crowd started to thin out. The water now was somewhat cooler as they waded into the on coming waves. She started to feel a bit chilly so they packed their gear and headed to the car. They walked hand in hand like a couple of teens in love for the first time. HER hand was so hot that BLAKE wanted to have sex with her as soon as they returned to his home on the water.

His beachfront was beautiful to look at but the waves reached generaly seven feet high making it nearly impossible to swim. They arrived at the beach house in a short time. HE parked the MERCEDES and they headed inside. They wasted no time getting to the bedroom. BLAKE took her gently by the hand and sat her down on the edge of the waterbed. She started to undress. She was naked in minutes and got into position for a sex romp. BLAKE was ready as usual wanting her so badly. IN minutes they were in a compromising position. Blake gave her his undivided attention. as much as she needed. She laid there waiting for the lust to take hold of her inner thighs. HER desires were at full speed.. They made love for a good hour then they rested due to exhaustion. Blake lit a cigarette as he returned to the bar and mixed two more drinks. IT was nearly five p/m now and the summer sun was hidden behind some large white clouds and a nice breeze off the ocean found its'way through the open patio door. IT was mother nature at her best.

BLAKE decided to shower as she dozed off on the lounge chair. HE thought about her and how they met and the hot sex. IN minutes he was turned on ready for more action from this hot babe that came into his life. Blake needed-her to relieve his anxiety and hot sex would be just the ticket. Even when she was half asleep she was still a hot bitch in the rack. Blake felt he had finaly found a new soul mate. IT had taken him a long time and many relationships to find a babe like this JOANNA, this goddess of love and lust. Blake had an enormous appetite for sex with women but also he swung the pendulum the other way with his male lover REX. Blake wrapped in a towel now headed in to bedroom. HE glanced at her for a moment not really wanting to wake her but her large breasts and her hardened nipples were to hard to resist.

HE moved closer to her now her naked body giving off warmth like a cat in heat. HE parted her legs and mounted her and in moments she awoke happily surprised by his sexual advances. She needed him as much as he needed her. She took a better position and as she moved he entered her deeper making her scream with joy. Sex with BLAKE was the ultimate she told him as he turned her over to gain rear entry to her waiting wet vagina. Blake was like a wild man now thrusting her as hard and as fast as he could wanting to satisfy her in every way that he could possibly do. She gyrated her body taking him inside her as deep as he could go. IN moments they had reached the point of no return and their love fluids exchanged with an impact driving her over the edge of reality. HER body was so hot to touch, her desires at their peak, her lips in need of a french kiss, and her legs wide open waiting for fullfilment.

BLAKE went for all of it taking her into fantastic bliss beyond her wildest expectations. She had never been so sexually alive as she was that night with BLAKE EDWARDS. HEwas indeed satisfying her every desire., her every need, emotionaly as well as her physical needs. They made love until exhaustion kicked in. They both laughed as the sweat from their bodies filled their bodies with moisture.

IT was surprising to both of them how well their desires blended. HE already knew that JOANNA was indeed in line to be MRS. BLAKE EDWARDS. She more than likely would say yes after all it was a chance to live a life of real money, hot sex, and happiness. She wasn't looking to marry to soon at all but if the right guy came along she might except the idea of settling down again.

BLAKE took a serious liking to her, thought she'd make him a good wife. IF she didn't work out he figured he could always kill her like the others. So far the former three wives were killed and he walked away a free man. HE felt that he had nothing to lose. And after all he still had REX his male lover who adored him as an alternate. They both sat and sipped their drinks relaxing in each others'arms. She felt comfortable lying naked in his muscular arms. HE enjoyed looking at her stark naked body, his eyes focused on her hairy vagina. HE placed his hand there running his long fingers inside her. She didn't budge but leaned back spreading her legs even wider now. She loved the attention he was giving her. HE was full of desireand mounted her quickly. IN a short time they went at it hot and heavy. She was getting sore and needed to stop but did not want to disapoint him. Finaly tired out they quit for a while. HE made two more drinks and in a short time they were drunk.

They finaly fell asleep in each others' arms. Morning sunshine peeked its' way into the room. THE warm summer breezes entered through the glass patio doors that had been open. The ocean roared against the rocky shore. The seaguls filled the air with their screeching sounds and their wings flapping in the morning air. IT was the start of a new day.

BLAKE awoke and slid from JOANNAS' grasp. HE headed to the bathroom to shower as she slept soundly on the couch. After showering he put on a pot of coffee, his morning ritual. She was still asleep as he lit a cigarette and poured himself a cup of coffee, HE opened his copy of the DAILY NEWS and scanned through it searching for his horoscope. HE like reading the horoscope even though he did not really believe in it.

She opened her blue eyes and searched the room for BLAKE. She now could smell coffee brewing and went to the kitchen. BLAKE gazed at her naked body as he kissed her cheek. HE was in the mood for a morning romp with his new found goddess of love. HE reached for her and in seconds wrapped his arms around her lifted her up and carried her to the bedroom dropping her gently on the king sized water bed. IN seconds they were in a compromising position and the adult sex games started once again setting fire to their ultimate desires. She was ready. willing and able to handle his sex advances. They made love for quite a while until the point of near exhaustion. HE could not believe the energy she had as she took him on with all she had to make his morning of bliss and one of harmony. They finaly had to break loose for a short rest. They laughed and joked carrying on like two teenagers.

HE thought about seeing her on a regular basis then popped the question. She responded with a yes. HE was happy that she accepted his offer. HE wanted her to move into his house on the beach. This to him would be the ideal situation that more than likely would lead up to a marriage proposal. Their relationship was moving at a rapid speed. BLAKE in the past always pushed hard and in this case he wanted her for himself not chance that she'd meet other guys. HE was planning in a short time to ask her to be his wife. How she would react to his request remained to be seen. After all she had no idea she was going to be wife #4. HE gave no thought to he being married before. TO him it was a new beginning, with a new babe who sexualy clicked with his own needs. They were truly compatible, there was no doubt about it.

HE had last after several affairs found true love once more. She put his pleasure first instead of her own needs. She was not selfish at all. She wanted to prove how much she was worthy of being with him. She had a feeling she found a guy who could give her the world at her disposal. She just felt she could be happy with him. HER deceased husband had been good to her and was quite a lover taking her sexual needs over the edge at times but he prematurely died of throat cancer. IT was a short marriage just made five years to the day of his death. Now she was starting over a new relationship entailed. She wanted a man in her life, happiness and money and BLAKE had it all. IT was was his move now. HE was wide awake now and he had a thirst for a dry martini. HE mixed her a drink as well as they made idle conversation. They sipped their drinks

Blake turned on the tv to the news channel. JOANNA was very quiet as he got the baseball scores. HE smiled at her when he heard that the YANKEES had won the afternoon gameHE was a big YANKEE fan since he was a small child and went to many games at YANKEE STADIUM with his dad over the yearsJOANNA liked the L/A DODGERS so they had similar interest in sports. BLAKE liked a woman who enjoyed sports. She was happy to share an interest in sports with him

BLAKE suggested they hit the beach since his home overlooked the ocean. She undressed and put on her bikini. BLAKE was getting hot looking at her standing there practicaly naked in a sense. HE was hoping none of his male neighbors would be on the beach this morning. HE didn't want any other man looking at his babe. HE was a jealous guy and kept his former wives under lock and key. His single male friends had great jobs, lots of cash, a big boat and a line of bullshit that most women would fall for. HE didn't know if she was easy to get to by guys who were so rich and handsome, smart and were looking for a quicky. HE wanted to trust her

IT was noon as they made their way down the wooden steps that led to the oceanfront. The breezes were warm, the sun was shining and the ocean was inviting them to take a plunge. IN minutes they were splashing each other and her breasts were bouncing up and down as she playfuly messed with BLAKE. HE loved looking at her body -for a woman over fifty she was dynamic looking and as guys would say a hot babe. She had breasts thet stood erect like a teenage girl and legs like a model and everything else fell into place topped of by a great personality and a smile that could melt the coldest mans' heart. She was unique and smart as well with a degree in physics.

BLAKE held her close to him as he noticed another guy placing his towel on the sand several yards from where they sat. HE was protective of what he considered his property. The guy waved to BLAKE who totaly ignored him. BLAKE was to interested in her more than anything else trying so hard to capture her attention. She seemed to like the beachfront. She paid no attention to the other guy. HER body was hot again for BLAKEand BLAKE only.

The sunshine beat down on the white sand making it uncomfortable to walk on so she remained in the water for the time being. BLAKE hugged her tight feeling her hot body so close to him ignited his loins and made his manhood pulsate teasing her intimate area. She pushed her body as close to as she could feeling his penis hard and throbbing against her. She was getting hot and wanted relief on his water bed as soon as possible. HE suggested they head back to the house. She agreed. Hand and hand they walked up the wooden staircase that led to the beach house. The sun now had gone down and the wind had picked up some causing a coolness in the atmosphere.

They reached the patio door and then suddenly he picked her up in the air and cradled her soft body protecting her to a degree. HE now carried her into the bedroom. HE placed her on the water bed and started to untie her bikini straps allowing her large breasts to jiggle loose with their nipples hard and protruding upward like minature pointers. HE started to squeeze her soft tanned breastswhich were hot to the touch. She moaned and placed one of his hands between her legs making her gasp for breath as his fingers searched into her crevice allowing her to moan even louder. HE smiled shyly as he grabbed one tit and sucked the nipple biting it until she screemed to stop.

HE now moved himself on top of her pulling at her bikini bottom to get them off her and tried to enter her begging her to open up her legs. She relaxed and let him enter her pussy. She was ready to satisfy his every need regardless that she was exhausted from the long day of activity. HE was ready to take her on and promised himself he'd give it his all even though his energy had truly been depleted. She laid back relaxed and ready to give herself to him like a virgin on her wedding night. HE french kissed her with a deep meaning, passion igniting her senses of her sexual needs. She gyrated like a cat in heat making him practically beg for the reward that awaited him. HE held back a little trying to tease her to some degree instead of just letting go and getting the act over with. She continued to gyrate giving him a chance to go deeper inside her to the point of releasing his sperm. HE kissed her deeply-his tongue finding its' target. She was hotter than she had ever been pushing herself as hard as she could to satisfy his animalistic desires.

AT this point BLAKE was ready to release but he was playing her game to build up to a dramatic climax which would take him over the edge. She had given him all the energy she could muster up to please him. HE could not hold back any longer and emptied his sperm into her big vagina. Her body shook as he took her to the next level of bliss. She gyrated like crazy as he french kissed her. Exhausted they both fell asleep.

Morning seemed to have arrived quickly. The sun was peeking through the venetian blinds, along with a nice breeze caressed the open windows. BLAKE was still asleep but JOANNA was already in the shower getting ready to start her day.

She admired her naked body in the full legth mirror. She felt proud of her figure, so youthful looking for a lady in her early fifthies she thought. She remembered how the boys always wanted to have sex with her as a teen back then. She had a figure that any guy would die for at least that was her own opinion. Now here she was a grown woman with needs especialy those of sexual in nature. She already felt that BLAKE was her soul mate. HE satisfied her in bed and that counted for something that's for sure.

A few months passed and BLAKE and his lover JOANNA dated heavily ending up at her place or his for sexual romps to top an evening off with. Blake moved her into his condo. They lived together for quite some time. Then one night he surprised her with a diamond ring and asked her to marry him. She never hesitated to say yes. They were married in a simple service at his condo. The justice of the peace married them on a SUNDAY afternoon and they had a small party with a few close friends to celebrate the occassion. THEN that night they flew out to L/A. for their honeymoon. They arrived 5 a/m L/A time. They took a limo to their hotel in SANTA BARBRA. They like being as close to the shore as possible. The hotel wasn't to far to travel too. The sun was rising as the limo dropped them at their hotel. IN minutes they were checked in and headed to their honeymoon suite. The room was extra large with two beds, two baths, a patio. a bar. all the comforts of home were there for the asking. The first thing on their agenda was to get naked and make love in these beautiful surroundings. BLAKE loved looking at her naked body. HE was fascinated by her beauty which made her look so much younger.

JOANNAS' big breasts sat up -no sagging there as he well noted to himself. She had cheerleader legs so much like a real young girl. This fascinated BLAKE making him want her so much that he could not get enough of her bountiful body.

She wasn't bashful in bed either always making it new and exciting for him. She was hot to the touch as they laid there across the kingsize bed. She seemed to have a boundless energy not quitting after a rough and tumble bit of sex. She wanted more and more from him. Whatever he could produce for her the more she took it into her deep womanhood. BLAKE gave it his bestshot. They spent the morning in bed having sex in every way feasible. She delivered with enthusiasm that sent him over the edge. They showered and dressed casual and headed to the food court.

IT was lunch time already. They got a table on the patio and ordered drinks first to celebrate their special day. The sunshine was conforting with a warm breeze off the ocean front. Seaguls played in the sky floating in the air like toy airplanes, diving for fish and other items of interest. JOANNA looked stunning in her turqoise colored blouse and tight black slacks that showed curves that would make any man envious of BLAKE. BLAKE wore a RALPH LAUREN navy blue sport coat, white shirt, and white slacks and a sailor hat looking like a ships'captain on an ocean cruise. They got all the attention as they took their seats at the white table facing the beautiful ocean. IT was a typical L/A day for sure as they made small talk that lovers do on their honeymoon while their eyes focused on each other and they held each others hands like two teens in love for the very first time.

The waiter took their order, refreshed their drinks as they were captured by their love for each other like no one else was in their magical world of blissThe waiter brought their entrees and they sat and fed each other like two love birds anxious to please each other. IT was a marriage made in heaven it seemed to them as they glanced at each other intently realizing they now were not only lovers but husband and wife as well. IT was truly a day for celebration. They chatted over dinner and made plans to play tennis, minature golf and swimming. They now finished dinner and ordered two more drinks. After two hours of dining BLAKE and JOANNA walked along the shore. The night was just beginning and a warm breeze filled the air. The full moon added a romantic touch as they strolled hand in hand along the boardwalk. IT was another perfect night in L/A.

The beach was crowded, with tourists, college kids on SPRING break and the regular natives enjoying as much of life as they possibly could. BLAKE and JOANNA were so wrapped up in their own world to take notice of others. IT was party time thats' for sure. IT was just about nine p/m when the hotel decided to have fireworks displayed. The fireworks created an atmosphere of pleasure and fun for all. People were cheering and applauding the spectacular fireworks displayed. BLAKE and JOANNA sat on a seawallof concrete enjoying the gala affair. The night breeze was soothing as the two lovers held hands enjoying the fireworks lighting up the sky. The fun lasted for hours then they went to the bar for a nite cap. The bar was noisy full of mostly college kids partying about spring break. BLAKE ordered for them, lit a cigarette and took her small warm hand and held it softly making her smile from the jesture. Several drinks later they headed for their room.

She was in the mood to make love but he extremely tired. She figured she'd tease him enough to set a pattern of the attention she craved for. She locked their door behind them and started stripping for him. HE paid little attention due to he was pretty drunk. She was feeling tipsy herself but liquor always had an adverse effect with sex as the relief so for her this was a very normal reaction to too much partying. She was in the mood but BLAKE just could not make the grade. HE did want her though.

He really wanted her badly, but his energy was depleted. HE had to much drink hindering his sexual performance. She was somewhat disapointed for she needed him so badly to make love to her. She had been horny all day, her sexual needs reaching their peak wanting him so badly. She undressed and stood naked in front of him but his attention was diverted by a bad headache from too much booze. She touched her breasts trying to entice him but nothing worked. HE could not perform and that was that. HE fell asleep smelling of booze cuddled up next to her naked waiting body. IN no time he was asleep as she laid next to him frustrated.

Blake slept soundly through out the night. JOANNA was really upset with him. She fell asleep next to him full of frustration. JOANNA would tell him what she thought as soon as he awoke.

Morning seemed to had come quick and JOANNA was up at the crack of dawn. BLAKE was still asleep, still reaking of beer. She was angry at him. She could not wait to give him an argument about his drinking and behavior. She was really pissed off with his drinking habit. BLAKE opened his eyes slowly, his vision sort of blurred from the hangover. HE could see JOANNA but her face was a mass of a blur and distorted from where he lay on the edge of the bed. She was standing over him now frowning like a mad dog hungry for a snack, ready to take a bite out of anyone or anything. She would even the score now no matter what the consequences prevailed. BLAKE had no idea what her feelings were about his drinking because she never said much to him about it. NOW even though they were newlyweds she was ready to tell him abou his drinking.

JOANNA remained quiet gathering her thoughts on how to approach him about his boozing all the time. She refused to tolerate his antics as much as she loved him it wasn't going to fly by her standards of decency. BLAKE argued that he had the right to drink if he so chose. Her opinion angered him to the max. HE was already angry enough to walk out on her. BLAKE was really deeply in love with her but would not tolerate anything that prohibited him from drinking. HE never could face the fact that he was indeed an alcoholic. HE often in the past denied his drinking habit. HE never would would plead guilty to too much booze. HE was getting irritable. She didn't back off, which iritated him even more. A major argument was about to explode. Blake had no problem arguing his point. HE had been down this road before with his other three wives, so certainly this was old news, nothing new. She was going to challenge him and his drinking habit, wheter he liked it or not. She would never back down. HE was getting agitated even more with her as she rambled on loudly not caring who heard the nasty words that were putting more stress to the situation. IT was going in the way of an explosive situation.

BLAKE always thought that his opinion of his drinking was not debatable because it was of his own choosing to drink and that was the bottom line. HE swore he would never take requests or orders, or commands from anyone in regards to his drinking, not even from his spouse. HE was going to have his own way of life style and tough on those who didn't like it. Blake was furious with her as she yelled at him. HE wanted to hit her. The more she yelled the more it reminded him of his three other wives who he had gotten rid of. Perhaps she would be dead wife number 4. Blake was now getting hostile almost to the point of out of control. She could see the fury in his hazel colored eyes, could read his special expression of hate towards her as she agitated him to the breaking point. She was not going to back down either was BLAKE after all he believed he was right and that she was wrong in her aligations about his booze habit. HE tried hard to tolerate her harsh words, but found it difficult not wanting to fight back at least verbaly.

He was trying to tolerate her but, found it extremely difficult. She was as much as a bitch as his former wives as far as he was concerned. HE wanted to hit her but decided not to after all they were newlywedsand he wanted this marriage to work. She finaly quieted down. HE reached out for her, tears now flowing from her eyes now shadowed a guilt on him which he found very hard to deal with. HE told her he was sorry for acting the way he did. She dried her eyes and then hugged him. HE was starting to sober up some. She was hoping somehow she'd get him to quit his drinking, IT would be in best interest to quit before he would develop a liver problem that could turn fatal. She wanted a perfect marriage which was not realistic of course. BLAKE had his drinking habit from when he and JOANNA started dating. She never suspected anything like this to ever happen. With BLAKE the relationship had started out with sexual compatibility. IT was hot sex that took their relationship to a whole new level. JOANNA wanted more than a bedroom routine. Blake wasn't quite ready for a real relationship for he had excess baggage from his other wives which he still did not tell JOANNA about yet. She was in for a rude awakening. They broke their embrace and Blake sat on the love seat next to her.

They talked about him going to a/a. HE was opened to that idea, felt he really didn't need help and that he'd get through this tough period in his life somehow or other and he asked her to be patient with him. HE begged her for her support and promised that he'd straighten out in due time. She said she'd support him as long as he cooperated and did the right thing to change his future.

BLAKE stood there looking at her as though he was seeing her for the first time. She held him close as tears fell from her eyes. Blake now tried to comfort her with the assurance that things were going to be fine from here on out. She wanted to believe him. She truly loved him but had her doubts that he'd quit drinking. HE had gone clean just before he met her and now he was slipping back once again. IT was a constant struggle trying to stay away from the booze. HE had very little will power. HE wanted to please her but on his own terms. Only time would prove wheter he could beat the addiction. She had her doubts but was willing to be supportive to him.

Two days later he was taken to the local hospital, his condition critical, his status a projected long time coma. HE had mixed his pain pills with booze nearly killing himself doing it. JOANNA was mortified, not knowing wheter her newlywed husband would die or survive and if he survived how was he going to function mentaly she wondered. She talked to the doctors who really gave her hardly any real hope that he'd make it. She sat in the I. C. U. unit waiting room crying and praying for BLAKES' recovery. This was the first episode with the coma according to the doctors it could last for months to come. JOANNA was finding this hard to deal with. IT was an emotional rollercoasterthe way things were going.

She had no one to turn too for support. She had no family there and no close friends to speak of. She was depressed trying to get through this turbulent time. She entered BLAKES' room and went close to his bed. The medical tubes and hookups to keep him alive frightened her terribly. HE virtualy was kept alive by a few machines. IT was up to GOD now wheter he'd make it or not. JOANNA sat there in a dead silence praying to herself that GOD somehow would let him live. She could not go on if something happened to him. They were only married several months and this hit. She had a hard time trying to struggle with these medical issues. She watched his monitors for hours praying things would change for the better. She met with the doctors on several occassions but they could not give her the benefit of good news. She felt hopeless and was starting to get depressed.

Several days later BLAKE woke from from the coma, She got a call from the floor nurse to come to the hospital right away that he asked for her. She was estatic as she drove there from their home. She could hardly wait for the elevator to take her to the tenth floor to his isolation unit. AS she arrived she put on a cap and gown and rubber gloves and signed the roster. HE looked up at her and smiled at her, IT was the first time he had smiled in ages. She touched his right hand feeling his warmth inspired her to cry. She continued to cry for they were tears of happiness. The head nurse attended to his needs and gave hope to JOANNA with words of kindness. She now held BLAKES' hand as he smiled trying to speak but the words were difficult to get out for some reason. The nurse entered the room to change BLAKES' i. v. bag. JOANNA sat quietly watching the monitors.

JOANNA was worried for he had not eaten in weeks and was showing signs of weakness. She felt this situation was like a real bad nightmare and she wanted it to go away. Over the next few days BLAKES' health had improved. JOANNA was pleased to see he could come home in a day or so as long as his improvement stayed on a steady keel. BLAKE was anxious to get home, he disliked hospitals, their atmosphere upset him. JOANNA told BLAKE to be patient that he would be home soon. A few days passed and BLAKE was released. HE was going to have some therapy at home from the visiting nurses' office in his town. His insurance would cover the cost for a total of six months only. At least it was a start on the road to recovery. BLAKE was glad when they left the hospital that morning. HE was anxious to get home -away from the doctors, nurses, the hospital itself. They drove the highway and were back at their place real quick. JOANNA helped her husband into the house. IN a short time he was asleep on the couch and JOANNA attended to preparation of supper.

She glanced at him checking periodicaly to make sure he was okay. BLAKE was resting comfortably. She smiled to herself and continued cooking. HE would sleep for a few hours at least until the sedatives wore away. HE was very weak yet and the doctors were not happy releasing him but, they did and BLAKES' health was on the line for he needed additional medical care but signed himself out which was legal but not in his best interest. BLAKE being real wealthy pushed others around to get whatever he wanted. HE was always brash, even as a youngster. After all his dad had owned several oil drilling companies and was worth billions of dollars far above the average oil millionaires.

BLAKE was duly spoiled rotten. He had an attitude, dated rich girls only while his friends' families struggled to survive. HE could care less. HE was rich the day he was born into the world. Blakes' parents were second generation rich. They were snobs and were disliked by others who lived in the upper class neighborhood. Blakes' parents always drove the best cars., had better jobs had the larger home, had the biggest sailboat as well. They had the biggest egos also. They were legends in their own minds. Blakes' made the Deans' List. Parents had the world by the ass. BLAKE had always gotten whatever he wanted. Being the only child he was the charming prince of his parents' home.

Blake grew up in an elite neighborhood. HIS neighbors were millionaires. HE attended expensive private schools. HE had the world by the ass as far back as fiftheen years of age. HE was your typical rich spoiled brat. HE had been educated at the best colleges too and made the deans' list when he had got into his twenties. Life was good for what ever he he needed or wanted was his and price was no object.

Even in college when other students struggled to make car payments he drove around campus in his brand new PORCHE. HE was a ladies' man even back then, even back in his college days but only dated the rich girls. Blake always had his choice of the most beautiful women. Now that was all behind him along with a a few bad marriages. Now life was different since JOANNA was chosen as his wife after so much dating prior brought bad results of heartbreak and cheaters. BLAKE was a hard man to please, his sexual appetite a little over the edge. HE had always been one with a sex appetite beyond what experts considered the norm.

After several love affairs JOANNA filled his needs for she was a woman with sexual demands most men she had dated could not handle. She was very sexual ever since she had discovered puberty at an early age of eleven. She had multiple lovers as early as that tender age, HER parents abused her so she sought the safety with male dominant figures. AS early as eleven she was sexualy active with guys eighteen and older, She liked variety. dirty sex. was her thing,

Over time she had gotten an older guy to get birth control pills from a drugstore owned by his father. His father encouraged him his son to have sex with JOANNA even though she had built a bad reputation in town. JOANNA was an easy target, She later got into drugs as well as prostitution, She had been arrested a few times but, put out for the vice cops, then they let her go with no arrest, She was a young girl learning the hard lessons of life on the street, She lived in her dads'abandoned car up behind the farmhouse where she grew up, The farm had been literaly destroyed by a ravaging fire,

Both her parents were killed as the fire burned out of control during an electrical storm. She somehow obtained a job as a waitress and got herself a place of her own in a flop house on the lower east side of town, She started going to college, taking night courses and finaly graduated with a associates degree in physics, After college she got a better job and moved to a better area away from the ghetto, AT her job she met BLAKE who was visiting a friend at the center where she worked, AS time passed BLAKES ' visits were more frequent and he captivated her. Later they dated and got married, The rest is history like the saying goes,

She as his wife was put on a pedestal by BLAKE and spending money on her was no problem for he had not even scratched the surface of the old money generated by his parents, JOANNA loved being queen and the more he pampered her the more she liked it, JOANNA made dinner as BLAKE napped, HE had needed extra rest because of surgery, HE also was mentaly exhausted from all the tests that were conducted, HE needed to rest for it would be a long time before he'd be on his feet again, Hours passed and JOANNA had not bothered to wake BLAKE, HE was still weak so she let him sleep, IT was going to take time for his body to heal,

HE slept pretty soundly as JOANNA got the dishes done and set aside plates of food for them for later, JOANNA looked at BLAKE lying there so peacefuly there not knowing her future was about to change, BLAKE had other plans that did not include JOANNA,

Unknown to JOANNA BLAKE had a girlfriend who was a nurse who had worked the floor when he was in the hospital, HIS new flame was half his age but he found nothing wrong with that nor did the nurse who had the hots for him. JOANNA had no idea that BLAKE had taken a lover and planned to get rid of JOANNA somehow even if it was murder he'd do it or have a hit man to get rid of her making it look like an accidental death possibly. He showed no remorse for murdering his former wives and after all she had served her purpose as far as he was concerned so to kill her was the game plan. so be it he figured, She didn't matter to him anymore, How to kill her was the question,

NOW with his lover the nurse he figured he had to get rid of her, BLAKE had many criminal friends who could kill his wife for a tidy sum, AS soon as he was well enough and back on his feet he'd make a few calls, Some of his buddies were professional hit menand others rigged cars with bombs or bad brakes. IT was up to BLAKE to decide how to say his last goodbye to his latest wife. Also he had to find her insurance policy which would pay him a cool million dollars upon her death. HE had placed the policy in a bank safe deposit box the day after they returned from their honeymoon. HE had so much to gain by her death. HE and his lover would then take a trip to TAHITI with the insurance moneyafter he had JOANNA creamated. Now as he stretched out on the couch smoking his expensive cigars he smiled to himself as he thought about the trip to TAHITI and the wild sex capades he and his lover would anticipate. JOANNA would be out of the equation so life once again change and he was use to change any way.

TO him JOANNA had served her purpose so be it he thought. And the important issue to him was how to spend the million dollars. HE had no remorse about killing her. She was just a mere chapter in his screwed up lifestyle. HE had always been a man to use and abuse a woman. His main goal was to have sex with them see if they were wife material, marry those who qualified and insure them and send them to a premature death and spend the insurance money. TO him life was a business deal awaiting conclusion. HE'D laugh all the way to the bank. Plus to eliminate any suspicion he insured the former wives with different insurance companies and this always worked out in his favor. NO one ever questioned him after all the premiums were paid off well in advance so no one cared if a claim was made. IT was all legal of course in his favor. HE had it made, he had a great game, and a great life.

This time he promised himself JOANNA was the last wife. For now he had plenty of money, HE had collected millions over the last so many years. Now him and his lover could enjoy life on the beautiful beaches of TAHITI. Blake could now shake his guilt partying with his latest love. Now all he had to do is make that one call and have JOANNA bumped off or set up an accident that would kill her. HE didn't care for this was all about money.

JOANNA had gone to bed so Blake made a call to a friend who would set up a plan to kill his wife. This time it would look like a home invasion with murder attached. His friend would make sure BLAKE would be somewhere else with a good alibi. HE then would break into Blakes' house making it look like it was a home invasion at random. He'd rape JOANNA and kill her and leave her naked body on the bed in the master bedroom. Then the killer would call BLAKE to tip him off. Blake would have all the bases covered. Now all B lake had to do was sit back and wait for the next day his wife would meet her death. Then the cops would be called, reports filed, the priest called for services, a quick creamation and then the smooth talking for the million dollar payoff. Then off to TAHITI for a month or so pleasure with his lover.

His lover was excited about heading to TAHITI with Blake. She really did not know that he planned to kill his wife. She assumed he got a quick divorce. Better she did not know his true reasons to get rid of JOANNA. All she cared about anyway was that she had found herself a sugar daddy. Now it was time to enjoy a new lifestyle with a man who was wealthy.

Blake packed his suitcases and his lover called and said she was ready to be picked up. Now they'd head out to the airport using a rented car so no one could trace his vechile. Meanwhile JOANNA was asleep in the master bedroom. Blakes' associate was just pulling up in front of his home when his cell phone rang. Blake was checking on him and wanted a call when the job was done. He paid out $10, 000 to the killer. HE figured the investment was well worth it for soon he'd file a claim with the insurance company and grab a cool million. Nice interest on an initial investment he thought.

The killer talked quickly as he entered the patio door. Blake told him to call when he was done so he could wire the $10, 000 to the killers' account in an off shore bank. They covered all the bases it seemed.

The hitman moved snake like as he went through the house. HE had been shown the house prior so he'd be able to get in and out quickly. HE came to the open door of JOANNAS' room. There she slept totaly nude which excited the killer even more. HE moved closer to the bed viewing her body in the dim light. She laid there so innocently as he fondled her breasts making her nipples hard quickly. HE grabbed her and laid on top of her as she awoke startled, screaming out as loud as she could. The killer choked her and in seconds she was dead. HE moved quickly now and headed for the sliding glass door onto the patio. HE closed the door behind him and headed down the walkway to the street to his car. HE drove away heading for the freeway. HE called BLAKE as he entered the ramp. Blake was glad it was over. HIS voice carried no remorse at all. Blake agreed that the money would be transfered by computer as soon as they reached the airport. This was fine with the hired killer. BLAKE knew he'd never screw this guy out of the money.

This guy pal of Blakes' had a lot of muscle behind him was an ITALIAN mob. They would not hesitate to give BLAKE a burial at sea. Those guys played no games. They were strictly business. They could care less who you were. IT was all about the money.

The traffic was light heading into the airport. Blake figured he'd turn the keys in at the car rental. Then they'd get ready to board soon for their flight to TAHITI. His new love had no idea what a mess she was getting into. The two previous wives death were still under investigation. The court already awarded BLAKE the settlements but the insurance company just didn't buy the whole story. They figured if they could prove Blake was lying they'd get him arrested for fraud and he'd be in jail forever. Blake never worried about anything legaly for he had a hot shot lawyer who had defended many rich and famous celebrities over the years. Blake had hired the best lawyer money could buy.

Now they had an hour delay on their flight. Blake and his lover went to the nearby cafe. They sat on the patio deck and watched the planes come and go. They ordered drinks and Blake pulled out his computer. She smiled not knowing what he was up to. HE moved cash from his savings account and wired the killer the money to an off shore bank. HE got verification quickly as the money changed hands. NOW the deal of getting rid of JOANNA was finalized. HE felt more relaxed now that his payment had been handled.

BY now he was thinking someone may have discovered the body. He had an alibi so he was off the hook. His witness was sitting right there with him. She had no knowledge of what he was up to so if she had to testify she'd be a great witness. She was with him for a reason besides sexual gratification that he needed from her. The flight was announced and they headed for the doorway to the airline. The line moved quickly and soon they were ready to enjoy a great vacation spot. The plane took off quickly. The flight time would be five hours so they made small talk and took a nap.

Meanwhile back at Blakes' residence a next door neighbor had discovered JOANNAS' body. The local homicide division showed and the local cable channel reporters. The story of her death spread quickly. The entire area neigborhood had showed up gawking trying to get a look at the corpse. BLAKES' phone rang and woke him up. HE recognized the number that of his brother. His brother explained to Blake what he had saw at the house. Blake told his brother he was on a business trip worth millions and could not return for at least a week or so. Blake told his brother he'd wire him money so at least JOANNAS' body could be removedto a funeral home. HIS younger brother agreed to finalize that end of it and that he'd call Blake the next day with the details. Blake promised to pay him a nice healthy sum of cash for his doing these needed things for him.

Blakes' lover BRENDA was asleep next to him. The more he looked at her the more he wanted to get to her in bed and satisfy his desires. She kept his attention. The flight now was coming into the air in TAHITI. She awoke and grabbed their carry on baggage. IT was time to depart the plane and head out to the carousel to get their other luggage. This done they reserved a limo at the service desk. Within an hour they were on the way to the hotel.

The air was balmy as they got into the limo. The driver loaded the suitcases and then put on the a/c which made it a lot more comfortable. The ride to the hotel was short and in a short time they were checking in. Again Blake checked out her slender body, her perky breasts got him excited. HE could not wait to make love to her. The porter showed them to their room. AS BLAKE opened the door he saw a large table with nice flowers and champaine. HE smiled and she did too. They dropped their suitcases on one bed and headed to the other bed undressing each other as they moved along. IN minutes they were in a compromising position. She moved her body like a wild woman keeping his interest intently. She was out of control it seemed as she climaxed with the upmost intensity. Blake was drained. IT had been a long day but she wanted more sex so he did his best to satisfy her desires. They made love for hours until he was totaly drained of energy. She was ten years younger so she had more stamina than he did. She took a deep breath as she slid from under him. She went to the bathroom to shower while Blake took a nap. HE was wiped out but satisfied by her sexual encounter. She took a nice long shower as her desires for more sex built up. She really loved Blake and wanted so much more of him than he could deliver at the moment.

She wrapped the white terry towel around her and headed to the bedroom where he was still asleep. She did not wake him but slid in next to him and covered up with the heavy blanket. The room was ice cold due to the a/c. She hit the lamp switch and settled in for the night. Morning arrived and he was up pacing the floor as he spoke softly on the phone with his brother. Somehow Blake had to send more money to do a creamation. HE took out his computer and sent his brother $3500. Brenda was moving about on the bed but did not wake yet. Blake promised his brother more cash for himself by that afternoon. HIS brother agreed to handle the funeral arrangements. HE also told Blake that the sheriffs' office was investigating JOANNAS' death. Blake had denied having anything to do with her death. They ended the call just as BRENDA woke up. She was hot and bothered and wanted lots of lovin. Blake was not really in the mood as she forced him down on the bed and placed his penis against her. Blake just could not get excited enough to continue would be difficult. HE tried to explain it to her but all she did was pull at him even more which made him angry. She felt hurt at first but tried to understand. HE finaly relaxed and apologized to her. They made passionate love for quite some time, then rested, making small talk. Blake got up from the bed and mixed them a couple of drinks. HE always needed a drink and a cigarette after he had sex. HE proposed a toast too them and their future. She smiled warmly as their glasses touched. Blake now remained quiet as he thought about the police investigation in regards to the murder of JOANNA.

Blake worried that somehow a neighbor might had got a glimpse at the hired killer as he entered his property. His neighbors were very nosey at times. HE had to distract BRENDA so he could call his brother again to get a update. HE had an alibi but if they caught the killer by some chance, the killer might confess the whole story to save his own ass. IT was a wait and see what happens next for BLAKE. Blake did not fear the law. HE was over confident, a showoff arrogent guy.

She had no knowledge of what made him tick. She was in for a rude awakening one day. The odds of the cops catching on to his game were in their favor not his. The companies not BLAKE. The insurance companies for some reason did not trust Blakes' testimony. IF they could prove he used fraud and murder to collect on he would more than likely get arrested and have to pay back millions. HE had gotten a few good payoffs but could care less about being investigated. After all he paid the premiums on the policies so he felt all in all this settlement was his and that was the bottom line.

The day went by quickly. Blake and BRENDA took a swim in the pool on the deck below theirs. The weather was letter perfect. The breezes were caressing their sun burnt faces. The sky was crystal blue in color. IT was just nature at its'best. The water temp was nice and comfortable as they splashed about like two teens in love. After a romantic swim they went to their room for a quick sex romp. She was horny and he was also. IT seemed the outdoors mother nature provided enticed them to catch up on their love life. They had sex until both of them were exhausted. She was completely satisfied, so was he. HE laid there close to her looking at her beautiful naked body. HE wanted her again but she had drained him of every drop of sperm she could get. Blake reached over and caressed her hard nipples. Her breasts were hot to his touch. She loved the extra attention he gave her. She was an attractive blond, young. about half his age, nice breasts. tight rear end and a decent loverwho seemed to have boundless energy.

Naked she laid there her womanhood covered in dark brown hair and was moist to the touch everytime he touched her there. She liked being fingered -it relaxed her. She could climax if he worked her clitoris. She was ready, willing and able when it came to hot sex. She had reserve energy for making love. Blake on the other hand was twice her age but could keep up to degree.

They finaly fell asleep in each others' arms. Hours passed and around midnight Blake awoke next to her. HER body was hot to the touch and Blake wanted her but would not wake her. HE lit a cigarette and laid there watching her sleep peacefuly. She was so young, vibrant gorgeous, well built, smart and had a great personality. Blake admired her. Plus she was a registered nurse, had a condo on the beach and a beautiful home in MALIBU, CALIFORNIA. HE had finaly someone who had it all. She also really cared about him. HE was different than any man she ever met before. Blake was rich, had a great way with women, was suave, a gentleman when he had to be, had a great smile and a line of shit that women adored. HE had it all. Women just took to him, he had some kind of majic power.

Blake loved all the attention the women gave him. The women treated him as though he were a GOD. HE knew how to pour on the charm when it was needed. Other men could not figure just what women saw in him besides his money. Now that all business was set aside Blake AND BRENDA headed downstairs to the lower restaurant. They were seated at a corner table a more intimate spot where they'd share more privacy. They ordered cocktails and revieved the menus. The waiter took their order and they sat there and made small talk. HE held her soft hand as he gazed into her hazel colored eyes. She could not wait to get back to their room for some sexual activity. She was in heat like a male cat ready to pounce the first chance he gotShe leaned closer and french kissed him. HE smiled as the waiter stood there with their drinks. Blake called a toast to their relationship. Their glasses touched as their eyes met. She smiled warmly as he sipped he sipped his drink. The meals came and they ate making small talk. She wanted to do some sightseeing and go to the beach for a swim. She heard there was a private nude beach and for a membership they could join the other people and soak up the sun. Blake did not like the idea that other men would see BRENDA naked.

Brenda wanted to expose herself for it was a turn on and the thought of seeing other men naked turned her on also.

AS she talked more over dinner she was trying to convince BLAKE perhaps he'd enjoy seeing lots of women lying there in the buff. HE felt his penis hardening as the thought about all the naked broads especialy the real young ones who claimed to be virgins but were not at all innocent. HEpromised to think about it. She had made up her mind that she was going to swim nude at that beach one way or the other wheter he agreed to it or not did not matter at all. She isn't married to Blake. BRENDA became quiet, she kept thinking about the nude beach. She would be willing to strut her stuff in front of as many guys as she could. Blake was not the type of guy to let anyone see him nude nor his lovers' body either. HEwas sort of a jealous lover kind of guy. They had dinner and left the nice place on the beach. HE suggested they'd take a drive up the coastline. She agreed to it but kept the nude beach in the back of her mind.

Blake drove slowly out of the parking lot and headed west along the shoreline. IT was still light out as they moved along enjoying the scenery. The main road was row after row of palm trees. The sky was crystal blue matching the ocean. Seaguls filled the air with their screeches. The wind was mild and warm as the evening was approaching. Blake was a bit moody as he thought about her suggesting a nude beach. AS he drove faster now his mind raced into a near rage as if he wanted to kill her. HE glanced at her with a warm smile. She smiled back. Blake took a deep breath and started to calm down. HE lit a cigarette and turned on the radio to a f/m channel hoping to get some soft music. HE was horny as he looked at her breasts so close yet untouchable due to he was driving. HE was tired now from the long drive and suggested they get a hotel room just for the night. HE needed her hot body and could not wait to much longer.

They drove for another half hour finaly saw a sign for a motel three miles off the main highway. Blake was glad he had to get his rocks off that were full of sperm at this point. She was in for a rough ride in bed chances are at least three times of hot sex before it would be over. The circular driveway was so inviting as they pulled off the main road. Blake pulled up in front of the office. The vacancy sign was lit. They went to the office, got a room and took the stairs to the second level. HE found the room and unlocked the door. The room was large and over looked the ocean. The patio doors were open allowing a nice warm breeze to enter. BRENDA closed the curtains and put on the a/c then went to the bathroom and undressed. She entered the bedroom naked. HE stood there admiring her body especialy her womanhood covered with a thick black patch of hair. Her nipples were hard and pointed upward as she moved now towards the bed.

Blake moved quickly now undressing as quick as he could. BY the time he was naked he had a nine inch erection ready to enter her bush in a heart beat. She laid there legs spread eagled her hair between her legs wet with desire as he crawled towards her wanting her so badly that he was ejaculating drips of sperm onto the sheets. She grabbed his cock and stroked it. She wet her lips with her mouth as she forced his nine inches into her waiting mouth swollowing at least half of his rigid cock. His tip of his penis throbbed in her mouth ejaculating his body fluids onto her tongue. She went into gyrations finaly begging for his hard cock to be placed inside her wet vagina. HE placed it there thrusting harder and harder until he could not hold back any longer and released his hot sperm into her waiting hole. She went gyrating like a cat in heat begging forever begging for more. HE gave her the balance of his load but had no more. However he was still hard so she gave him another good long hot blowjob. HE came this time off in her mouth making her gag and she spit up on the sheet. HE was all smiles as she continued to lick his balls down to his crotch making his balls hard and sore. She then jerked him off looking closely at the tiny hole in his tip as fluid still stringy protruded from his hot cock. She was so hot that her body gave off radiant heat. She wanted more of the same. She turned on and there was no turning her off. Blake tried desperately to perform but just could not make the grade.

They rested for a brief moment. She being younger had vibrant energy which seemed endless. HE told her to roll over on her stomach and to spread her legs giving him entrance to her rear end. IN seconds he had an erection and pushed it hard into her anus dripping sperm all over her legs. She moaned for more and he gave it his best move and shot a load into her rear end making her yell out loud that she needed even more of his gooey white sperm. She was sweating like crazy now trying to get off once more with great difficulty. She gyrated taking him deep inside her as she groaned like a bear. Blake could not believe her sexual peaks. HE had lots of women but no one ever as hot as this bitch. She could make love for hours without a breather. HE could not get over her energy level, then again she was half his age so he was not one to complain.

He loved how she moved her body especialy what she could do with that big hairy pussy of hers.

Meanwhile back at the house his brother let the police in to finish searching the place for clues to JOANNAS' murder. They now were searching through her personal stuff. Oddly enough they found a cassette tape with a note attached. The note explained that if was found dead this tape would point the finger at the guilty party. She also had a diary they found under her bed. The diary pages were full of info in regards to Blake and how she heard him planning someones' murder possibly hers as she overheard him on his cell phone one afternoon when he thought she was asleep. Now the police could swear out a warrant on BLAKE as a person of interest in relation to JOANNAS' death. The cops said nothing to his brother about what they found. His brother knew how to find BLAKE. HE would have to cooperate with the cops or he'd be held for further questioning and may even be a suspect himself. Blake had a solid alibi but the tape and diary might be enough to hang him for the crime.

IN the meantime the insurance companies had private eyes working on the case for they were trying to build a case against Blake. Sooner or later they'd get him. HE would more than likely stand trial for at least three murders. BRENDA had no idea what a mess she had gotten into. She was in for a rough time.

The police left Blakes'place and his brother locked up the house. HE called Blake to let him know the police had come back again. Blake was not a happy camper. HE was still waiting for the check from the insurance company for a cool million dollars. His beloved JOANNA was worth a nice sum of money. Also she had left a will leaving him a fortune in stocks and bonds that Blake never knew about. Plus she had taken out a life insurance policy for a million dollars payable to Blake if she became deceased. HE had no knowledge about this small fortune. IF he had played it straight with her all this could have been his free and clear. Now his destiny was undetermined. HE more than likely rot in jail.

Blake and BRENDA headed down to the pool. The area was crowded with tourists. HE found a table on the deck and grabbed the waiter and ordered drinks. BRENDA took off her shirt exposing her bikin top that held her large breasts. Blake looked her over as she removed the towel from her waist exposing her tanned shapely legs. HE was a bit jealous as guys walked passed and eyed her luscious body. BRENDA just took it in stride that guys looked at her over after all she had a body to die for like the saying goes. Blake was jealous as he watched the guys eyeing her. She was knock out gorgeous. She did love the extra attention she got though for it made her horny especialy looking at the guys in their tight swim suits that showed what they had that could be hers just for the asking. She loved mens' bodies She got turned on looking at the bulges in their swimsuits. She knew very well what they could do with their cocks that would satisfy her hot pussy.

Blake was certainly not her first lover. She had been a gang banger for years for a group of motorcycle guys. She put out for anyone as long as they could keep up with her sexual needs. She was far from being a virgin. She lost her virginity to her step father when she was thirteen and had an abortion at fourteen. She was a whore most of her life but seemed to like that way of life. IF BLAKE knew her background he'd more than likely dump her or kill her even if he was in that kind of mood.

They now shared drinks on the viranda soaking up the sunlight along with the warm breezes that patterned themselves.

After a while she suggested a shower and then some romping on the water bed. They went back to their room -locked the door and undressed quickly. She rubbed his cock for a couple of minutes turning it to a full nine and a half inch erection which delighted her. They entered the bathroom where she kept playing with his large balls loaded with sperm ready to shoot off. She picked up the toilet seat and jerked him off for a few minutes and his load hit the toilet bowl and his tip was wet and throbbing which now at this point got her so excited that she started giving him a blowjob as she fell to her knees. HE blew a second load off in her mouth making her gag and she spit up into the toilet the sperm still on her cheeks and lips. She grabbed the mouthwash and swished the green minted taste around in her dirty mouth. She did not get angry about the load in her mouth for during the time she ran with the gang she'd blow three to five guys one after the other until she puked her brains out. She swollowed enough sperm to fill a goldfish bowl. Now they stepped into a cool shower to cool off some. HE took a bar of soap and wash cloth and started to soap her hot body. HE washed her breasts and her nipples were erect -very hard to the touch. HE was getting an erection. IN moments he had his cock up her ass as he forced her to bend over. She grabbed his balls from behind squeezed them real hard forcing sperm to ejaculate in her anus. She loved it.

The more she bent over the easier to enter her vagina even though his cock was upside down in her vagina. She pulled it deeper inside her grabbing his balls again wanting every drop of sperm she could get.

His penis was now getting quite sore after so much sex with her these last four days. She said she was going to to get her period that night but she'd jerk him off or give him a suck job to clear his balls of any built up sperm. HE was glad for that. AS long as his big puffy balls got emptied it was fine with him. She washed off his cock with soap and the wash rag. Then she got down on her knees and sucked almost his whole cock. She was really into it which drove him over the edge of reality.

She was down right dirty. The night ended with pure exhaustion and they fell asleep in each others' arms.

The next morning BLAKE got a call from his brother again. This time it was real bad news. This time the F. B. I was there and forsenics also. This time Blake was a person of interest though they had no warrant for his arrest. HE was scared now more than ever. The color of his face alerted BRENDA that something was wrong. She didn't ask questions. She just sat there figuring he'd explain things if he wanted to. Blake sat there motionless as he hung up the phone. Inside he was shaking from the reality of the whole situation. She tried to smile at him but could not bring herself to do so. HE was quiet for quite a while-then got up and poured two drinks for them. His hands shook as he handed her a glass of sherry.

Blake now had started thinking how to get rid of her and head to SOUTH AMERICA where he had friends who could hide him out. HE figured he could put something in her drink so she'd fall asleep. HE had sleeping pills and when she went to the bathroom he dropped one in her glass and then fill her glass to the brim again. She returned to the room and sipped at her wine. After an hour or so she got real drowsy so he laid her down on the couch. He covered her with a blanket. HE made a few phone calls to his friends in SOUTH AMERICA. IN a short time he had driven to the airport not realizing he was being followed. The F. B. I. had tapped his line so they traced him right to the hotel. They figured they'd pick him up at the airport. After a few miles Blake turned into the airport parking. HE turned his rental car in and in minutes the F. B. I. picked him up. HE was now detained by them on suspicion of fraud and a few murders. The F. B. I made arrangements with an airline to fly him back home to the states. AN hour later they were in the air heading for the U. S. A. Blake knew the game was over.

Hours later he was brought to the F. B. I. office for questioning. Blake finaly after eight hours of questioning broke down and confessed to JOANNAS' murder. HE was formerly charged arrested and incarcerated. A trial date was set within two weeks from the day. Time went by slowly then the trial date came. Blake was transported by special U. S. MARSHALS AS they pulled up to the court house BLAKE figured he'd escape even though he had handcuffs on. HE waited close to the rear door. AS a marshall opened the door he kicked the marshal in the head and made his way on foot down the street. The other marshal spotted him ordered him to stop but BLAKE ignored it and kept running. The officer pulled his his service revolver and shot Blake in the back of his head killing him instantly. Blake had met his destiny. JOANNA in a sense had duly testified from the grave bringing Blake to justice.

CPSIA information can be obtained at www.ICGtesting.com
Printed in the USA
BVOW05s0040070414

349802BV00001B/26/P